Empty the ashtray.

Skin deep,

Left still rippling,

All the emotions held deep within.

Waves crash,

Laughter collapses.

Time embers our flame,

Struck from two matches,

Like the cherry burning holes in the couch,

Until we are left coughing up smoke.

2021   *poetry by Phoenix*

Dust is what becomes us.

Pebbles topple from walls of rock,

Statues chip, loved paintings fade.

There's permanence in the idea of love.

One that stays on a changing play,

When allowed, she will age.

When encouraged, she will change.

If nurtured, she will flourish.

Until the heartbeats of her fade.

A Gentle Mind on Fire

The tribute to madness,

We know,

All work.
No play.

Keep at work,
Keep your mind at bay.

No work,
Health would stay,

Then who would work for slaves' pay?

Play a while,
Inner Child awake,

Tomorrow is never a promised day.

2021   poetry by Phoenix

A Gentle Mind on Fire

Take the day.

Wind dancing across skin,

Rippling like red sheer fabric,

Turning and cascading in fluid movements,

As if to say

"Breathe easy, and allow yourself to rest today."

Wind relaxes,

Leaves stop their fall,

Even time itself encourages rest for all.

2021   poetry by Phoenix

A Gentle Mind on Fire

Set a goal.

To reach a goal,

Takes countless tries.

It takes countless hours.

Countless nights.

To reach a goal,

Is to accept you're not right,

To reach a goal, you must cry.

To reach a goal,

You'll have to fight,

But reach the goal,

You will some night.

2021   poetry by Phoenix

A Gentle Mind on Fire

Trials by fire.

Burn the witch,

We've heard it before,

As soon as you walk in freedom,

The crowd stomps outside your door.

Pires built faster than homeless are housed,

Sooner or later,

These petty fires will burn the whole fucking thing

Down.

2021   poetry by Phoenix

A Gentle Mind on Fire

Rotten.

It smells like something has rotten,

Curled up into a corner to be forgotten,

Left out of sight,

Out of line,

Flowers wilting and molding into the night.

Anxiety.

2021   poetry by Phoenix

A Gentle Mind on Fire

I see,

I see you with my eyes,

I see you standing wide outside the lines.

I see you carefully calculating what you'd think.

What you'd say if you needed something to drink,

What you'd do if someone asked something of you.

I see you.

The latest apology.

2021   poetry by Phoenix

A Gentle Mind on Fire

I am sorry,

Sorry for the way I changed,

Sorry for the pain,

Sorry for the acts i've done,

And the ones I had turned away.

I'm sorry for the lies I told,

To make you go away.

I'm sorry for the littlest things,

So sorry.

Every day.

The kind.

2021   poetry by Phoenix

A Gentle Mind on Fire

I am not the kind,

To sit around,

To play fine,

Mess with me,

Shake my might,

Mess with me,

But leave my mind.

Becoming grounded.

2021   poetry by Phoenix

A Gentle Mind on Fire

What breaks your knees,

When you've fallen down.

And is there for you,

When you are left to drown,

What buries you deep,

As you're laid to sleep,

And covers you

Compact enough to protect you unlike before.

A child lost,

A mother born,

Until I am covered by the dirt,

My heart will remain sore.

The messenger.

Dow   2021   poetry by Phoenix

A Gentle Mind on Fire

Would you hold my head,

When my thoughts leave it for dead,

When the light in my eyes refuse to shine,

Would you think twice about giving me your time?

When my smile fades,

And my tongue goes sharp,

Not all is lost,

It's just,

A broken heart.

I was Baptised

2021   poetry by Phoenix

A Gentle Mind on Fire

Fear is not love

I mutter furiously

Shoving my crayons into a box

And my feelings back behind locks

Love is not faith

I sigh instead of pray

Sundays always taste the same

And I feel like I should be ashamed.

Fear is not love,

Reflecting in my dreams,

Breaking cycles while I sleep,

And bringing new waves from deeper seas.

2021   poetry by Phoenix

A Gentle Mind on Fire

Wolves traveling

in packs of two or three,

Hunting,

stalking,

quietly.

They are always watching me,

Trying to see where

my hiding spots may be.

2021   poetry by Phoenix

A Gentle Mind on Fire

Echoes

There was a tapping on my mind

In the back Somewhere hard to find.

A haunting voice like a ghost in white.

Screaming something vicious about rights.

And screams, they echoed, throughout the night.

Until I found that tapping,

Looked at it in spite,

And begged it to explain why it was ruining my life.

A cackle became what screams once were,

The fact I remained stupidly thinking intentions

were pure.

2021   poetry by Phoenix

The Finding

When I met myself,
It was cold and dark.
I tried to speak out with words,
But i only ever got for a reply was heart.
A soft beat or two
And then it'd all but stop.
Waiting for a reply,
But I was left in shock.
I spent so long searching for myself,
That when I finally found them,
I felt like I was peeking into a shell.
Not one like on beach sands,
Colorful and soft.
No this one was different,
It was flesh,
But it was off.
I held myself together,
Tighter than before.
And spoke a little softer,
Knowing that it was sore.
I spoke kinder words,
I spoke with truth and remorse.
My body kept on beating,
And I learned to return.

2021   poetry by Phoenix

A Gentle Mind on Fire

My mind-

My minds a runaway train.

It's here for a moment,

Then it's off again.

It's been years since it left the tracks.

I've all but stopped trying to put it back.

My mind is a wild bird.

So skittish and so free.

It longs to fulfill its curiosity,

But once you're close itll fly and flee.

My minds a wilting flower,

Still attached to its healthy bush.

In its moment of glory,

And probably overlooked.

My minds a simple traveler,

She always packs so light.

As not to be so heavy,

That's the job of life.

2021   poetry by Phoenix

Essence

The dissolving memories of younger times,

Carving out space to try and redefine,

A minds physically burdened by weight,

And with time,

Those weights aren't only yours..

They're also mine.

An echo of much simpler times.

A cascade of tears that never dried.

Some laughter that caused cracked walls,

The anger that it caused,

the ivy that grew through,

The dulling of so many saws.

The essence of this place,

Ripples through the halls,

It reminds me of the art museums,

With its morbidly stale air,

And all.

Mourning coffee

I'm not addicted,

Those words taste bitter sweet.

I wake every morning,

Making some coffee to "eat".

I'm not addicted,

I try to convince.

I'm tired by noon,

And force swallow more sips.

I'm not addicted,

I whine into the night,

It's just my busy mind,

That's why I can't sleep right.

2021   poetry by Phoenix

A Gentle Mind on Fire

Words as weapons

Is is not what you said.

It's what you didn't.

Apologies left unspoken,

And doubts drown into my head.

It's not the sharp lashing of your tongue.

It was the well versed soft lies

Reflecting furiously

the damages they had done.

It wasn't the truth that kept me near,

It was the bruising on my knees,

And the bleeding in my mind.

Your words were weapons,

Edged with venom,

And I was just another victim.

2021   poetry by Phoenix

A Gentle Mind on Fire

Interactions

It doesn't take more than one moment,

One glance,

One statement.

To turn a heart around.

You've got its attention now.

But what do you do with it?

Best to let the moment pass,

At least until the lapse of creative conversations pass.

On that chance,

You've let a single opportunity rest.

Leaving and endless amount of

What ifs,

In its wake.

2021   poetry by Phoenix

A Gentle Mind on Fire

When in Rome

They say Rome,

Was not built in a day,

But whos to say it wasn't.

At least in romulus' eyes,

His city was already towering to the sky.

But built in battle and betrayal,

She was.

Everyone always forgets Rome's main currency was blood.

So when you build your empire tall,

Don't build it with the iron from those you felt are small.

Your city will crumble,

Greed will spread,

And before you can apologize.

Stabbed 26 times in the back,

They'll pronounce you dead.

2021   poetry by Phoenix

A Gentle Mind on Fire

Tsunami

Its in the shallow fast recoil of the waves,

That you have finally found a moment to behave

And in sorrow your apologies made wakes,

But they were nothing compared to the impending wave.

Of title proportions,

Making its way,

faster and faster

within minutes we wait.

As it crashes around,

That once shallow, now deep grave.

Ill reflect some thanks,

For the minimal effort you had made.

2021   poetry by Phoenix

A Gentle Mind on Fire
Plath

Inspirations are a source.

An ever plagiarized refreshed use of verbs.

Like the use of yellow,

And how that color disturbs,

Ever fragile minds,

And ever fragile worlds.

I found my warriors call one night,

I hide under my covers holding a light.

I read your poems,

Out of love,

And fright.

And then I shut my oven off,

And chose to fight another fight.

A Gentle Mind on Fire

war

Heroes aren't created,

Legions are left to die.

Then the one returning,

Well, they claim all the rights.

The gold, the women, the city.

The towers into the sky,

Heroes aren't created.

Only heroes ever die,

Wrapped in words so hollow,

Meant to give them might,

But there's no cause so noble

To force a man to bet his life.

2021   poetry by Phoenix

A Gentle Mind on Fire

A very special thank you, for purchasing my poetry. This is my first published piece of literature. It is a collection of poems written over the course of 2019-2021.

I'd like to take a moment to thank those in my life closest to me, the support of my friends and chosen family is unbelievable.

To my son Rowen, for giving me an excellent excuse to be a better me. In a world full of hate and distance, choose compassion and acceptance.

The content of this book does reflect mental health issues. If you are ever in a moment of crisis, please never forget. You are strong for seeking help, just try, one more time.

Suicide hotline for America:

800 273 8255

Made in the USA
Middletown, DE
03 September 2022

72020121R00015